Rocks in His Head

By
Carol Otis Hurst

Pictures by
James Stevenson

GREENWILLOW BOOKS
An Imprint of Harper Collins*Publishers*

Rocks in His Head
Text copyright © 2001 by Carol Otis Hurst
Illustrations copyright © 2001 by James Stevenson
All rights reserved. Printed in Hong Kong
by South China Printing Company (1988) Ltd.
www.harperchildrens.com

Watercolor paints and a black pen were used for the full-color art.
The text type is Original Garamond BT.

Library of Congress Cataloging-in-Publication Data

Hurst, Carol Otis.
Rocks in his head / by Carol Otis Hurst;
illustrated by James Stevenson.
    p.   cm.
"Greenwillow Books."
Summary: A young man has a lifelong love of rock collecting
that eventually leads him to work at a science museum.
ISBN 0-06-029403-5 (trade). ISBN 0-06-029404-3 (lib. bdg.)
[1. Rocks—Collection and preservation—Fiction.]
I. Stevenson, James, (date) ill.   II. Title.
RZ7.H95678 Ro 2001   [E]—dc21   00-056197

First Edition 10 9 8 7 6 5 4 3

For Keith and Jesse,
and all the others with
rocks in their heads — C.O.H.

For Wina and John — J.S.

Some people collect stamps. Some people collect coins or dolls or bottle caps. When he was a boy, my father collected rocks. When he wasn't doing chores at home or learning at school, he'd walk along stone walls and around old quarries, looking for rocks. People said he had rocks in his pockets and rocks in his head. He didn't mind.

It was usually true.

When people asked what he wanted to be when he grew up, he'd say, "Something to do with rocks, I think."

"There's no money in rocks," someone said.

"Probably not," said my father.

When he grew up, my father decided to open a gas station. (People called them filling stations then.) My grandfather helped him build one on Armory Street in Springfield, Massachusetts.

They called the station the Antler Filling Station.
My father carefully painted the name right over
the doorway.

Inside the filling station was a desk with a cash
drawer (which my father usually forgot to lock)
and a table for his chess set.

My father built narrow wooden shelves on the
back wall and painted them white. People said,
"What are those shelves for?"
He said, "I've got rocks in my head, I guess."
Then, one by one, he placed his rocks and minerals
on those shelves. He carefully labeled each rock to
show what kind it was and where it had come from.

In those days lots of rich people had automobiles, but then Henry Ford came out with the Model T.

That was a car many people could afford. My father had taken one apart and put it back together again and again until he knew every inch of the Model T. He thought that anyone who had spare parts for the Model T and could repair it so that it drove like new would do a good business. He bought some parts from dealers and found some parts in junkyards.

The pile of Model T parts sat just to the left of the lift. Soon, that pile of parts was bigger than the filling station.

People said, "If you think people are going to buy that junk, you've got rocks in your head." "Maybe I have," he said. "Maybe I have."

But people did come to buy that junk. They came to
buy gas and they came to play chess and they came
to look at the rocks.

For a while my father was too busy for the chess
games. He was pumping gas, changing tires, and
fixing Model Ts.

"Where did you get this one?" a customer would say, holding up a rock.

"Found it in a slag pile in New Hampshire," he'd say. Or, "Traded for it with a fella from Nevada. Gave him some garnets from Connecticut."

"People in Nevada and Connecticut collect rocks like you do?" people would ask.

"Lots of folks have rocks in their heads," said my father. He'd dig into his pocket and take out a rock. "Take a look at this one."

Then the stock market fell. At first, people didn't think it would matter much to my father. After all, he had no money in the stock market.

"I may have rocks in my head," he said, "but I think bad times are coming."

And bad times did come. People couldn't afford
to buy new cars or fix their old ones.

When business was slow, my father would play chess with some of his customers. When business was very slow, my grandfather would mind the filling station, and we'd pile as many of us kids as would fit into our Model T, and we'd hunt for more rocks with my father.

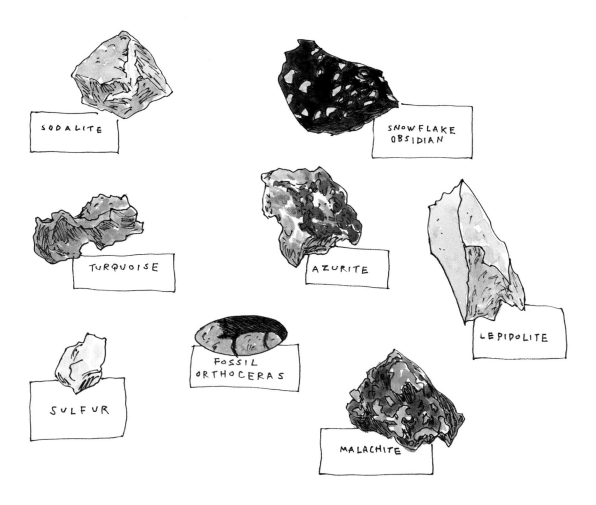

SODALITE

SNOWFLAKE OBSIDIAN

TURQUOISE

AZURITE

LEPIDOLITE

SULFUR

FOSSIL ORTHOCERAS

MALACHITE

He had to build more shelves for the rocks, up the west wall of the station.

Then people stopped coming for gas. They stopped coming to play chess, and they even stopped coming to look at the rocks and minerals. They were all too busy looking for work.

One day my father picked up the chess set and carefully packed it in a big box. He took down each mineral, wrapped it in newspaper, and carefully placed it in a wooden box.

When his friends came with a truck to help us move, they said, "Watch out for those wooden boxes. He's got rocks in his boxes, now."
"Yessir," said my father. "That's just what I got in there. Take a look at this one."

The house we moved to was old and falling apart.
My father said he'd have it fixed up in no time.

But before he started in on the repairs, we had to take those rocks up to the attic, where he'd already built tiny little wooden shelves.

My father did fix up the old house, and after he finished each repair, he went up to the attic with his rocks. He spent a lot of time reading about rocks, too.

"If you think those rocks are ever going to do you
any good," said my mother, "you've got rocks
in your head."

"Maybe I have," said my father. "Maybe I have."
He reached into his pocket. "Take a look at this one."

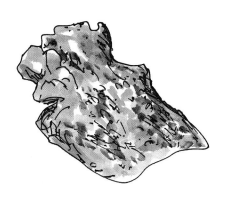

My father spent a lot of time looking for any job
he could find. Most jobs lasted only a day or two.

On rainy days when my father could find no other work, he'd take the bus to the science museum. They had a whole room full of glass cases containing many rocks. Sometimes he'd spend the whole day in that room.

One afternoon he looked up to see a lady standing beside him. "I've seen you here before," she said.

"I come here a lot," he said. "I guess I've got rocks in my head."

"Tell me what you're looking for," she said.

"I'm looking for rocks that are better than mine," he said.

"How many did you find?" she asked.

"Ten," he said.

The lady looked around at the hundreds of rocks, in all those glass cases. "Only ten?"

"Maybe eleven," he said.

He smiled. She did, too.

"You *have* got rocks in your head," she said.
"I'm Grace Johnson, the director of this museum.
These rocks have come from all over the world."
"So have mine," said my father. He reached into
his pocket. "Take a look at this one," he said.
"Did you study rocks at college?" she asked.
"Couldn't afford to go to college," he said.
"Let me see the rest of your rocks," she said.

Mrs. Johnson got out her big Packard touring car,
and my father got in. They drove to our house.
"Where are the rocks?" she asked.
"Up here," said my father, leading the way
to the attic. "Watch your step."

Two hours later Mrs. Johnson said,
"I can't hire you as a mineralogist.
The board won't allow it.
But I need a night janitor
at the museum. Will you take the job?"
"Will I be cleaning rocks?" he asked.
"Sometimes," she said.

So my father took the job as night janitor at the
museum. Before he went home, he'd open some
of the mineral cases and scrub some of the rocks
with a toothbrush until they sparkled like diamonds.

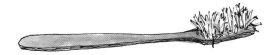

Mrs. Johnson came in early for work one morning and
saw him carefully writing a new label for one of the rocks.
"What are you doing?" she asked.
"One rock was labeled wrong," he said.
"I fixed it."

Mrs. Johnson smiled. "I've been talking to the board of directors. They know that I need a person here who knows as much about rocks as you do."

"What about the college education?" he asked.

She said, "I told them I need somebody with rocks in his head and rocks in his pockets. Are you it?"

"Maybe I am," said my father. "Maybe I am."

He reached into his pocket and took out a rock. "Take a look at this one," he said.

K-SPAR

MUSCOVITE

SPHALERITE

HEMATITE

CALCITE

QUARTZ

FLUORITE

PYRITE

GARNET